The Glass Bead Bracelet

Story by Jill McDougall
Illustrations by Tanisha Cherislin

Contents

Chapter 1

Something Special

"Ouch!" cried Bethanie.
"Mum! You're pulling my hair too tight!"

"Oops ... sorry," replied Mum.
"That's the last braid, I promise."

"Your hair looks amazing!"
said Bethanie's older cousin, Koko.
"Now we can put our costumes on!"

Bethanie and Koko were getting ready
to dance in a parade
at the African Festival in the city.
They were both very excited.

Before they left home, Mum said to Bethanie,
"I have something special for you to wear at the festival."

She was holding a beautiful bracelet with colourful beads of blue and green.

"This was my grandmother's bracelet," said Mum. "I brought it with me when I came here from Ghana in Africa."

"I'll take good care of it," promised Bethanie, as she slipped the bracelet on.

Chapter 2

Dancing in the Parade

An hour later, Bethanie, Koko and Mum arrived at the city square where the festival was being held.

People in colourful costumes were gathering in the square.

Koko spotted some girls from their dance group near the African drums.

“Good luck,” said Mum to the girls.
“I’ll meet you back here at three o’clock.”

Bethanie felt butterflies in her stomach as she joined her dance group in the parade. Would she remember all the steps?

But once the music started, Bethanie began to enjoy herself. She listened to the beat of the drums as she danced around the square.

At the end of the dance, people clapped and cheered.

But then Bethanie noticed something terrible!

Chapter 3

Nowhere to Be Seen

Bethanie looked down at her arm and let out a cry. The bracelet was gone!

"Koko," cried Bethanie. "I've lost the bracelet!"

Koko looked shocked. "Oh, no!" she said, frowning. "We have to find it!"

Bethanie and Koko searched the ground carefully,
but the bracelet was nowhere to be seen.

Lots of stalls had opened
and the square was more crowded than ever.

"I'm afraid it's gone," said Koko.

Suddenly, Bethanie caught sight of something on the ground near a colourful stall.
"I think I see it!" she cried, hurrying across the square.

Bethanie was soon disappointed.
It was not a bracelet on the ground after all.
It was a string of beads.

Chapter 4

New Glass Beads

The woman at the stall saw Bethanie
holding the beads.
"Thank you for finding those and picking them up,"
she said, smiling.
"They must have fallen from my table."

The woman seemed very friendly.

"I've lost something, too," Bethanie told her.
"It's a glass bead bracelet from Ghana.
My mother let me wear it for our dance today."

"I'm sorry you lost it," said the woman, kindly. Then she said, "Would you like me to show you how to make a new bracelet for your mother?"

"Thank you!" cried Bethanie.
She turned to Koko and asked,
"Do we have enough time before we meet Mum?"

"Yes," said Koko, looking at her watch.

The girls sat down with the kind lady
and she showed Bethanie how to thread glass beads
onto a piece of string.

When the bracelet was finished,
Bethanie looked at it in delight.
"This looks great!" she said. "I love it!"

Chapter 5

Two Special Bracelets

At three o'clock, Bethanie and Koko met up with Mum.

"I'm so sorry, Mum," said Bethanie.
"I lost your bracelet during the dance.
But a kind lady helped me make a new one."

Mum tried to smile when she saw the bracelet.
"Thank you, Bethanie," she said. "It's beautiful."

Bethanie could see Mum's disappointment
that her special bracelet was gone.

Bethanie felt miserable!

Just then, one of the girls from the dance group came rushing over.
She was holding something in her hand.

"Bethanie!" said the girl. "Did you drop this bracelet? I found it in the square!"

"Yes!" cried Bethanie. "That's my mother's bracelet!"

"Thank you for returning it!" said Mum, smiling at the girl.

Mum slipped the bracelet on her arm
and Bethanie put the new bracelet on her own arm.

"Now we both have a special bracelet!"
said Bethanie, smiling.